STAR WARS™

MEET THE HEROES

R2-D2

STAR WARS™

MEET THE HEROES

R2-D2

Written by
Emma Grange

What language does R2-D2 speak?

What was R2-D2's bravest mission?

Does R2-D2 ever run out of power?

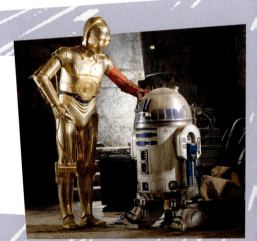

How does R2-D2 defend himself?

Can R2-D2 swim?

Find out the answers to these questions and many more inside!

Who is R2-D2?

A friendly droid.

Droids are machines that are **built** and **programmed** to work for others. R2-D2, also known as **"Artoo"**, is **happy to help** people!

Are there other droids like R2-D2?

Yes! R2-D2 is an **"R2"** unit. All droids are given **numbers** to identify them. These numbers are a bit like **names.** Here are some others!

R4-G9

What sort of droid is R2?

An astromech droid.

These droids are built for use in **space.** They work on starships, where they **fix** controls, **target** enemies and use mathematical calculations to help the pilot.

R4-P44   R5-D4   R4-P17

Where does R2-D2 come from?

A factory called Industrial Automaton. Droids are all built to behave the same. R2-D2 is different. He has developed **his own personality.**

Interrogation droid

Labour droid

Who uses droids?

Everybody! There are lots of jobs across the galaxy that only droids can do. The **evil Empire** uses droids. The **rebels** use droids to **fight the Empire!**

Waiter droid

Battle droid

Communications droid

How big is R2-D2?

Not very big. He is just under one metre (3 feet 3 inches) tall. Here he is with young **Anakin Skywalker,** one of his many friends.

What tools does R2-D2 use?

Lots! Droids are fitted with clever **technology** and **gadgets.** Inside his metal body R2-D2 hides a **welder,** a circular **saw** and many other useful tools.

Periscope

Grasper arm

Feet with
wheels

11

Can R2-D2 fly?

Yes! R2-D2 has **powerful rocket boosters!** The jets provide enough power for him to soar **above the ground.** This way he can travel to places his legs cannot reach.

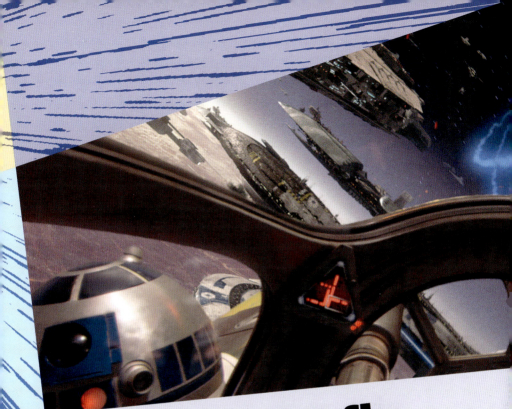

Does R2-D2 fly starfighters?

Sometimes! R2-D2 helps navigate starfighters through space. However, his main job is to **repair** any **damage** to the ships. He also acts as **co-pilot,** working with whoever is in the cockpit.

13

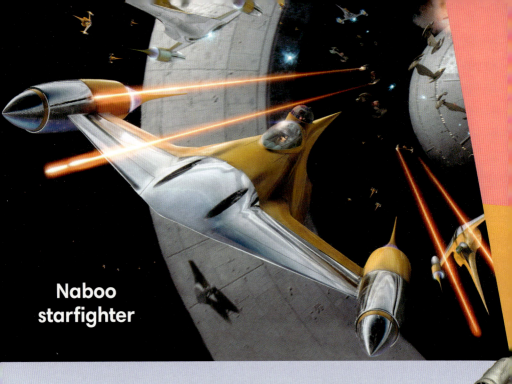

Naboo
starfighter

Which ships has R2-D2 flown?

Lots! R2-D2 has flown **famous rebel ships** such as **X-wings** and **Y-wings.** He has helped his Jedi friends Yoda and Anakin in their speedy **interceptors.** You can also spot him in a **shiny yellow** Naboo starfighter!

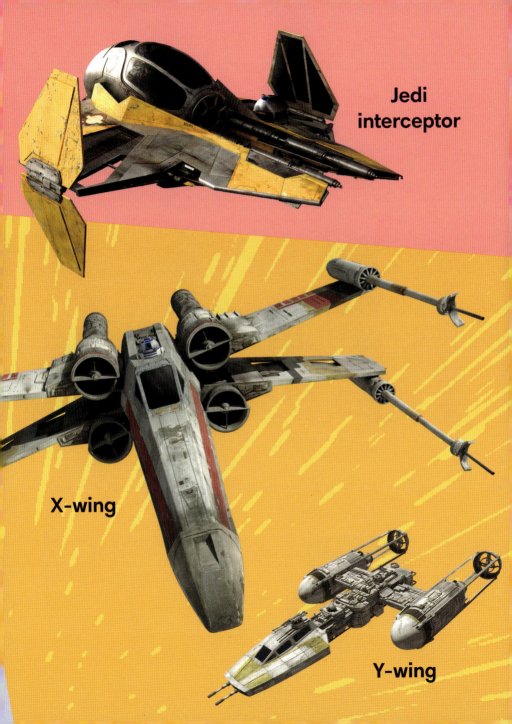

Jedi
interceptor

X-wing

Y-wing

Who has owned R2-D2?

Lots of people. R2-D2 has served two royals, **Queen Amidala** and her daughter, **Princess Leia.** He has worked for **Jedi Anakin Skywalker** and his son, **Luke Skywalker.**

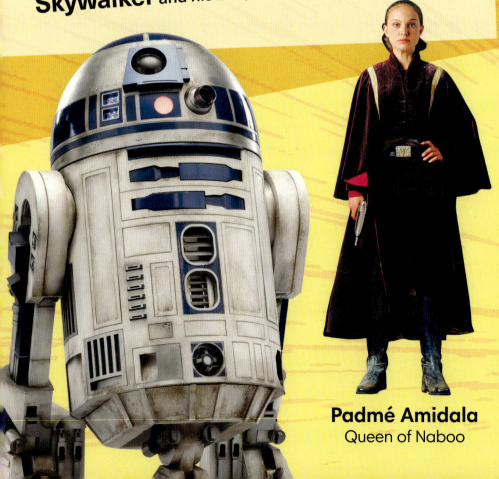

Padmé Amidala
Queen of Naboo

**Luke
Skywalker**
Jedi

Leia Organa
Princess of
Alderaan

**Anakin
Skywalker**
Jedi

Who are R2-D2's friends?

He has many. R2-D2 meets amazing friends all over the galaxy. Some of his friends are humans like **Luke Skywalker.** Some are **aliens** like **Chewbacca.**

Princess Leia
Human

Luke Skywalker
Human

Does R2-D2 have other droid friends?

Of course! R2-D2 has many droid friends. They include the ball-shaped droid **BB-8,** and the golden droid **C-3PO.**

Chewbacca
Wookiee

BB-8
Astromech droid

C-3PO
Protocol droid

19

What language does R2-D2 speak?

Binary. This is a special language used by computers. R2-D2 speaks using **beeps** and **whistles.** He understands many more languages, too.

How long can R2-D2 remember things for?

Forever! Some droids get their memories wiped to make sure they forget **secrets.** However, R2-D2 has **never** had his memory wiped.

Who can understand R2-D2?

His closest friends can.

Others can tell from his tone when he is **happy** or **telling a joke.** He uses loud noises or jumps up and down to let his enemies know if he is **angry!**

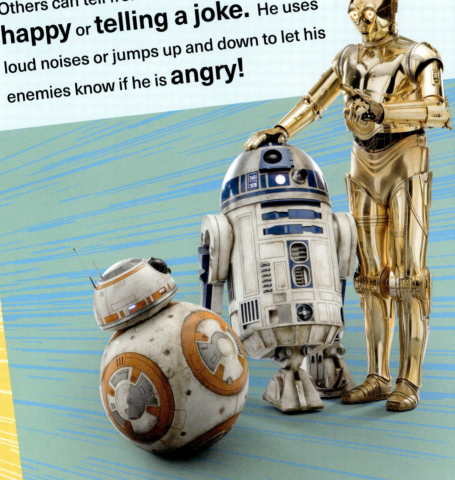

How does R2-D2 see?

With his photoreceptor.

The circle in the centre of his head acts as his **eye,** also known as a photoreceptor. His head **swivels** all the way around so that he can see in **all directions!** He also has extra **scanners** and **periscopes.**

Photoreceptor

Where does R2-D2 meet C-3PO?

On the planet Tatooine. C-3PO is a **protocol droid** built by young **Anakin Skywalker.** Anakin is very good at fixing machines, vehicles and droids. C-3PO often needs to be fixed!

Are R2-D2 and C-3PO best friends?

Yes! R2-D2 and C-3PO have been on many **adventures** together. They **understand** each other and can often be heard talking to each other. Sometimes they **tease** each other, too.

Does C-3PO always believe R2-D2?

No! R2-D2 often **surprises** C-3PO. On one trip, C-3PO thinks that R2-D2 will not be able to fix the equipment on-board the ship *Millennium Falcon*, but he's wrong. Silly C-3PO!

Yavin 4

Naboo

Hoth

Tatooine

Mustafar

Which worlds has R2-D2 visited?

It's impossible to count!

R2-D2 travels wherever his owners ask him to go. He has visited **fiery** planets full of lava, such as Mustafar, and **beautiful** worlds of fields and seas, such as Naboo! He can often be found at a rebel base, such as the one on Yavin 4.

How does R2-D2 get his friends out of trouble?

By always being there! When his royal friend **Padmé** falls into a moving vat that is about to be filled with melted metal, R2-D2 is there to rescue her. He **switches off** the machine just in time!

Can R2-D2 hack enemy systems?

Yes. R2-D2's **technical skills** help his friends plan their missions. He assists in a rescue mission against their enemy General Grievous. By projecting an image of Grievous's ship, the *Invisible Hand*, R2-D2 is able to show all the **escape routes.**

Has R2-D2 ever been to a wedding?

Yes! R2-D2 once worked for Jedi Anakin Skywalker. Jedi are not allowed to get married. When Anakin married Padmé Amidala at a secret ceremony, R2-D2 and C-3PO were the **only guests!**

What battles has R2-D2 been in?

Many. A battlefield is **no place** for an **astromech droid,** but R2-D2 is friends with people who often **get into trouble!**

Where was R2-D2 in the Battle of Geonosis?

Fixing C-3PO! R2-D2's clumsy friend is always getting into **scrapes.** Luckily R2-D2 is on hand to put his broken friend back together again. He must **work fast** and avoid enemy **battle droids.**

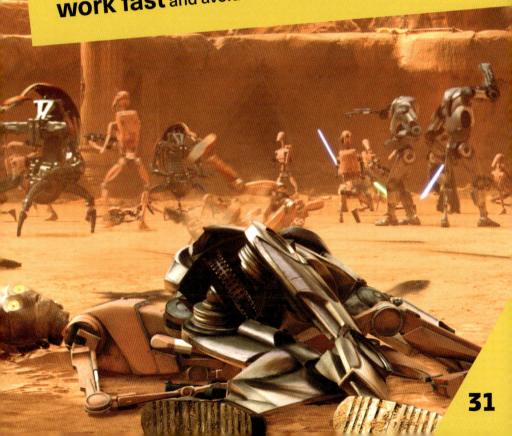

How does R2-D2 escape danger?

By using clever tricks! In one fight he lets off a **cloud of smoke** to hide himself and his friends. Their stormtrooper foes **cannot see** through the thick smoke, so everyone is able to escape!

How does he distract his foes?

With loud noises and bright lights! He lets out high-pitched **whistles** and crackling, flashing **lights.** This causes a **distraction** that helps R2-D2's Jedi friends escape. Their foes do not like the noises!

How does R2-D2 defend himself?

With slippery oil! When he is caught by super battle droids, R2-D2 doesn't use his sharp tools. Instead, he releases **black oil** from his metal body. The oil is **slippery,** making the bigger droid drop him!

Is he useful in a fight?

Yes. R2-D2 is good at **multitasking.** Whilst helping to fly Anakin's starfighter, R2-D2 fights off a **buzz droid** attack at the **same time!** The buzz droids have scary **saws** and **pincers!**

Can R2-D2 beat bigger droids?

Yes! R2-D2 knows that **size doesn't matter.** He may be small but he is **clever** and has more brain power than bigger droids!

Super battle droid

35

How does R2-D2 save a queen?

By showing great bravery. During a battle above the planet Naboo, Queen Amidala's starship becomes damaged. R2-D2 is the **only droid** able to fix the damage. He must dodge enemy fire **at the same time!**

37

Does R2-D2 work for the Rebellion?

He does! Some droids are programmed to be bad. But R2-D2 works for **rebels.** The rebels want to stop the Empire from controlling the galaxy. **Loyal** R2-D2 never abandons his friends on their dangerous missions.

What was R2-D2's bravest mission?

R2-D2 goes on lots of missions.

He is very trustworthy. Rebel Princess Leia once gave him a vital **message** to **keep safe.** He had to act in secret and transport the message.

How does R2-D2 escape the Empire?

In an escape pod! R2-D2 and C-3PO **eject** themselves into space in this **small vehicle** during an important mission. The Empire is trying to find them and **capture** them, but R2-D2 won't let that stop him.

What is a hologram?

A special type of picture. Droids use computer **technology** and **blue light** to project holograms. They can be used to send **messages** or to help people **communicate** with one another.

What message does Princess Leia give R2-D2?

A secret one! Leia **records** a special hologram message for Jedi Obi-Wan Kenobi. It is R2-D2's job to **play** Obi-Wan this message. Leia appears in the picture, as if she was really there!

42

What else can R2-D2 project?

Maps! R2-D2's rebel friends often ask him to show them hologram maps of the **whole galaxy.** Then they can see where their enemies are, or how to travel to **faraway planets.**

Who wants to sell R2-D2?

Jawas! These creatures are **scavengers.** They gather up and sell all sorts of scrap for money. They also **sell droids!** They think someone on their planet Tatooine will **buy** R2-D2.

Where does R2-D2 meet Luke?

On Tatooine. Luke works on a moisture farm on this sandy planet. When he needs new droids to **help him** on the farm, he thinks R2-D2 looks **useful.** He's not wrong!

Can R2-D2 find his friends?

Of course! When R2-D2 **loses** his rebel friends he uses his computer skills to **find** them. They've fallen into a trash compactor! He stops them from being **squashed,** then breaks down the door to free them!

When was R2-D2 scared?

When his friend Luke went missing on the snowy planet Hoth. There the snow was so **deep** that R2-D2 could not go out looking for him. He had to use his **sensors** to hunt for his friend.

Can R2-D2 swim?

Sort of! On a mission to Dagobah, R2-D2 falls into a **swamp.** His circuits are shielded against water damage, and he is able to **float** his way out of danger.

Has R2-D2 ever been captured?

Sadly, yes. Poor R2-D2 becomes the prisoner of slug-like **gangster Jabba the Hutt**. He is used as a **drinks trolley!** However, R2-D2 is soon able to escape. Clever droid!

What does R2-D2 hide for Luke?

His lightsaber! R2-D2's chest contains secret compartments. They are perfectly sized for storing Luke's weapon. When Luke is in trouble, R2-D2 launches his lightsaber toward him. **Catch,** Luke!

Has R2-D2 ever been used in a test?

Strangely, yes.

On the swampy planet Dagobah, R2-D2 is surprised to become part of some **Jedi training.** Old Jedi Master Yoda challenges Luke Skywalker to use the power of **the Force** to make R2-D2 **levitate!**

What is the Force?

A powerful energy. The Force exists in all **living things.** Jedi learn how to use it **for good.** As a droid, R2-D2 cannot use the Force.

Has R2-D2 ever been given an award?

Yes. After a big battle, the rebels succeed in destroying a key weapon belonging to the Empire. R2-D2 takes part in the **victory celebrations.** The rebel leaders recognise the important part he played in helping them **win.**

How does R2-D2 cope with sand?

With difficulty! R2-D2's **feet** are made of **treads** and **little wheels.** These treads are designed for **all terrains,** but rolling across sand dunes is hard work! **Keep rolling,** R2-D2!

Does R2-D2 like the cold?

Not really. If it's snowing a **blizzard,** even R2-D2 struggles to see. And a big **gust** of **wind** could make this little droid **topple over!** On frozen planets such as Hoth it's safer for R2-D2 to stay indoors.

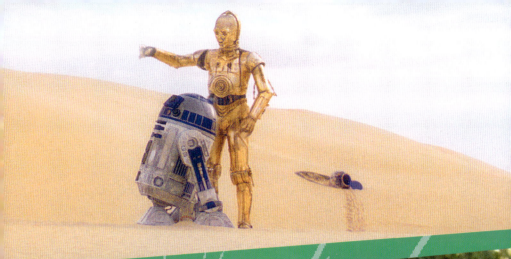

Has R2-D2 visited forests?

He has. On the forest moon of Endor, R2-D2 finds himself travelling up into the **treetops!** R2-D2 is not scared of heights, and thinks the forest is pretty. But he prefers to be back on **solid ground.**

What happens when R2-D2 meets the Ewoks?

He is very quickly surrounded!

These furry creatures want to protect their homeworld. They think that R2-D2's friends are a **threat,** so they tie them all up. Plucky R2-D2 **cuts** his friends **free** with his tools!

Does R2-D2 ever run out of power?

Yes. R2-D2 is sad when his good friend and master Luke Skywalker goes **missing,** so he turns himself off. Everyone **gives up** trying to fix him. Thankfully he wakes up all by himself!

Finn

Rey

What's next for R2-D2?

More adventures! The Empire has been defeated by the rebels, but a new evil power, called the **First Order,** threatens the galaxy. R2-D2 still has many **old and new friends** who **need his help!**

General Leia

Poe Dameron

Glossary

Blizzard

A heavy snowstorm with strong winds.

Empire

A group of nations ruled over by one leader, who is called an Emperor.

First Order

An organisation that takes control of the galaxy when the Empire is defeated.

Gangster

A member of a gang of criminals.

Jedi

Someone who uses the Force to protect people and keep the peace.

Levitate

Make something rise or float above the ground.

Lightsaber
A sword-like weapon with a glowing blade of energy.

Multitask
Do many different things at the same time.

Navigate
Plan and direct the route of a ship, aircraft or spacecraft.

Protocol droid
A robot who helps with communications.

Rebel
Someone who rises up to fight against the current ruler.

Scavenger
Someone who searches for and collects discarded materials.

Terrain
An area of ground.

Senior Editors Ruth Amos and Emma Grange
Senior Designers Lynne Moulding and Clive Savage
Project Art Editor Jon Hall
Designers David McDonald and Stefan Georgiou
Senior Pre-production Producer Jennifer Murray
Senior Producer Jonathan Wakeham
Managing Editor Sadie Smith
Managing Art Editor Vicky Short
Publisher Julie Ferris
Art Director Lisa Lanzarini
Publishing Director Simon Beecroft

DK would like to thank: Sammy Holland, Michael Siglain, Troy Alders,
Leland Chee, Pablo Hidalgo and Nicole LaCoursiere at Lucasfilm;
Chelsea Alon at Disney Publishing; and Lori Hand and
Jennette ElNaggar for editorial assistance.

First published in Great Britain in 2019 by
Dorling Kindersley Limited
80 Strand, London, WC2R 0RL
A Penguin Random House Company

10 9 8 7 6 5 4 3 2 1
001-314783-May/2019

A CIP catalogue record for this book is available from the British Library.

ISBN: 978-0-24138-774-0

Printed and bound in China

A WORLD OF IDEAS:
SEE ALL THERE IS TO KNOW
www.dk.com
www.starwars.com